Bruno Munari's

# ABC

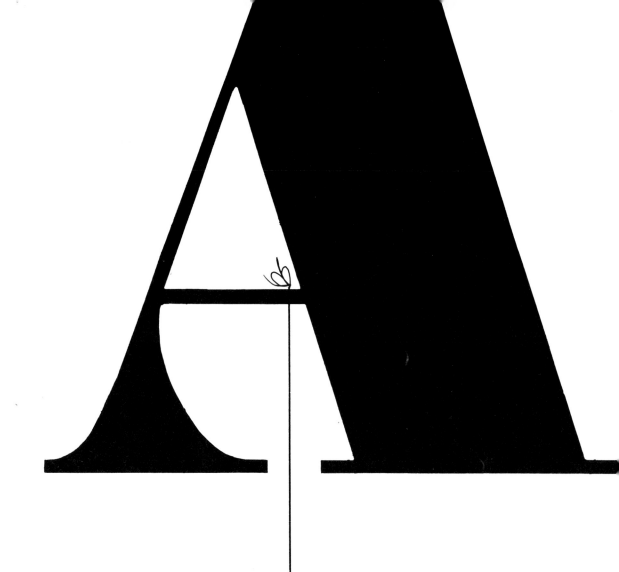

## An ALA Notable Children's Book

"A lighthearted alphabet book, full of the surrealistic surprises that one has come to associate with this Italian artist. . . . It is as if every letter had produced its own mood and color."

—The New Yorker

"With clean lines and brilliant full-color work, Bruno Munari's 'ABC' is at once unconventional, yet childlike, modern, yet timeless. A bold and refreshing kind of ABC book . . . Highly recommended."

—Library Journal

"Here is beauty and imagination and fun. No child should miss it."

—The Horn Book

by
Bruno
Munari

PHILOMEL BOOKS
NEW YORK

First paperback edition published 1982 by Philomel Books,
a division of The Putnam Publishing Group, 200 Madison Avenue, New York, N.Y. 10016.
Published simultaneously in Canada by General Publishing Company, Limited, Ontario.
Original hardcover edition published 1960 by The World Publishing Company.

Library of Congress Cataloging in Publication Data
Munari, Bruno.
ABC.
Reprint. Originally published: Cleveland,
Ohio : World Pub. Co., 1960. (Munari picture books)
Summary: The letters of the alphabet are
introduced by words and pictures beginning
with each letter.
[1. Alphabet] I. Title. II. Title: A.B.C.
III. Series: Munari picture books.
PZ7.M9232Aab  1982  [E]  81-19950
ISBN 0-399-61201-7 (lib. bdg.)   AACR2
ISBN 0-399-20884-4 (pbk.)

# A

an Ant

on an Apple

E

a Blue Butterfly

**B**

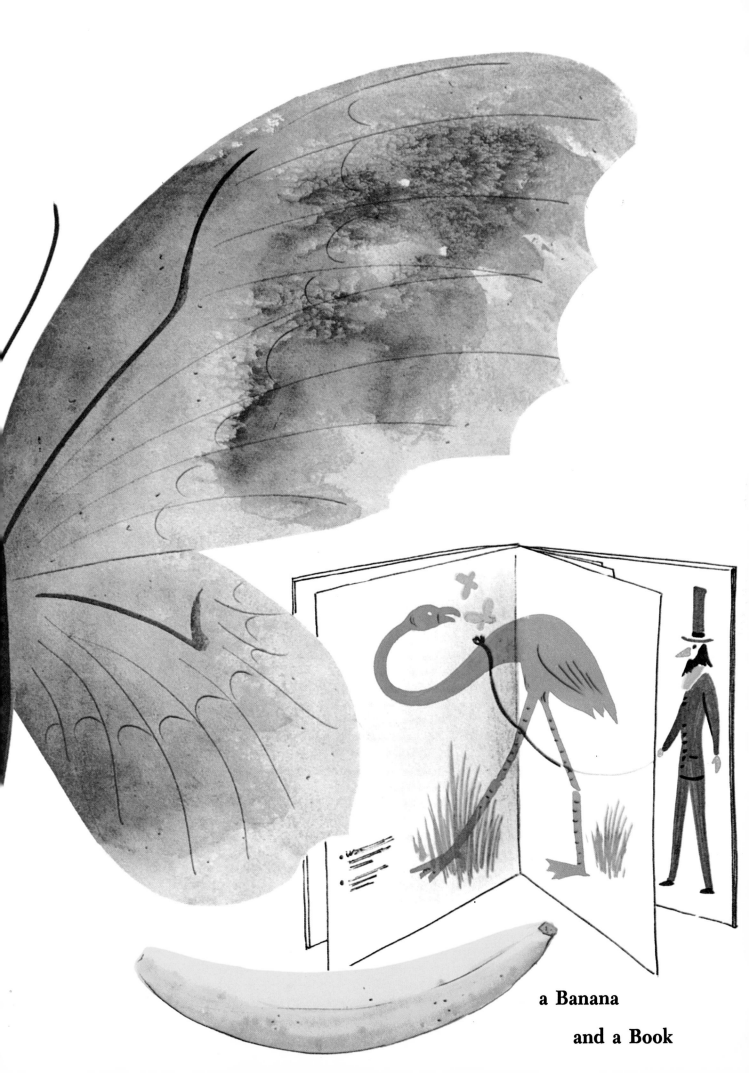

a Banana

and a Book

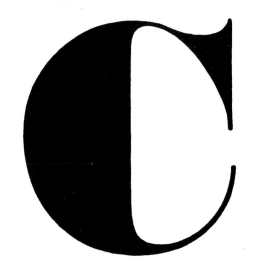

a Crow

on a Cup

a Candle

**and a Cat in a Cage**

a Drum

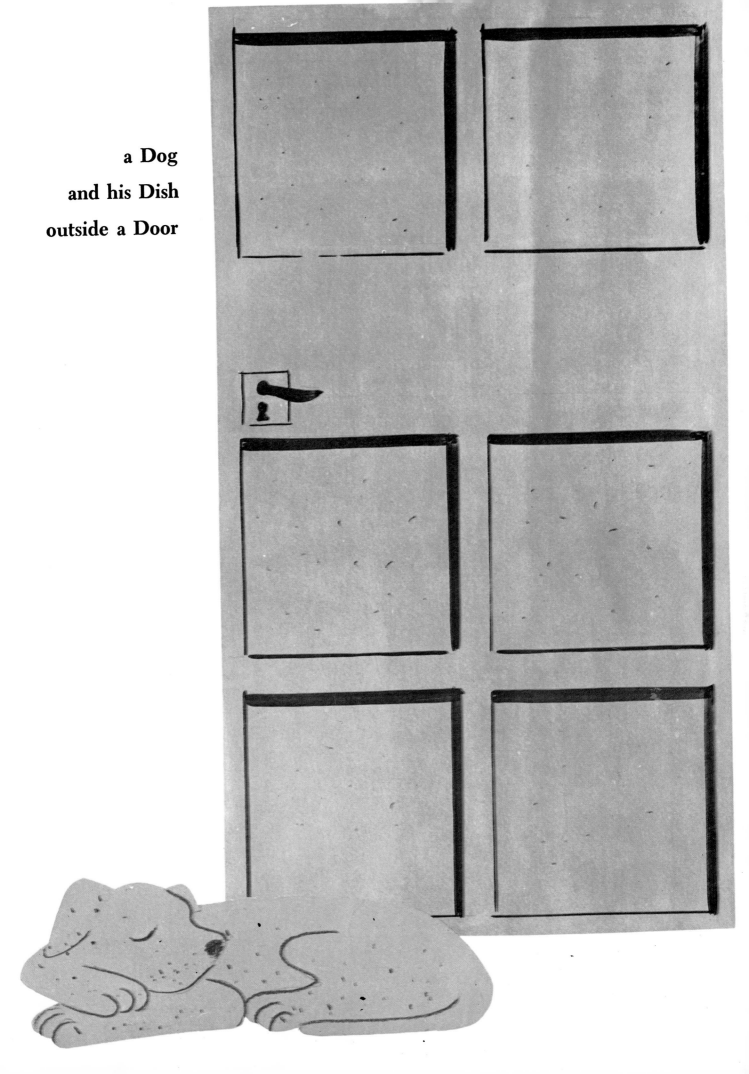

a Dog
and his Dish
outside a Door

an Elephant

an Egg

an Eye
and an Ear

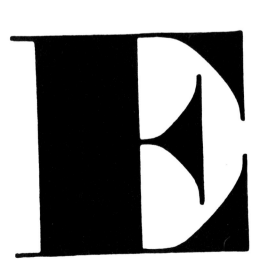

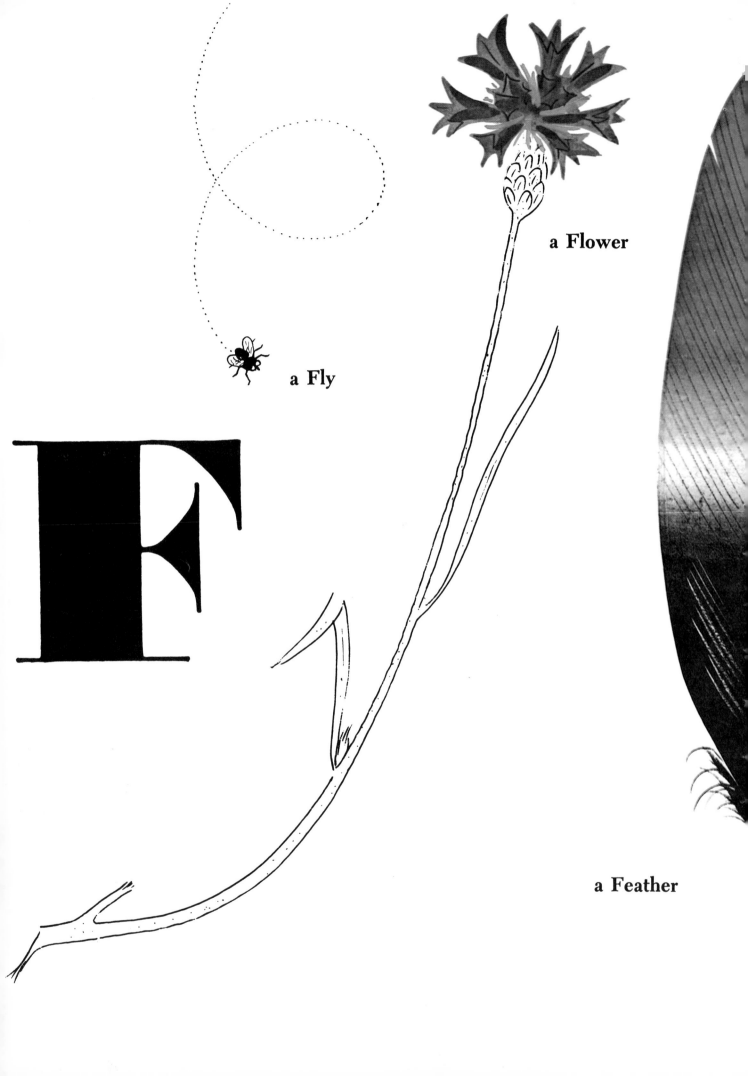

a Flower

a Fly

F

a Feather

more Flies

and a Fish

# G

Glasses in Green Grass

*still another fly!*

and a Gift for you

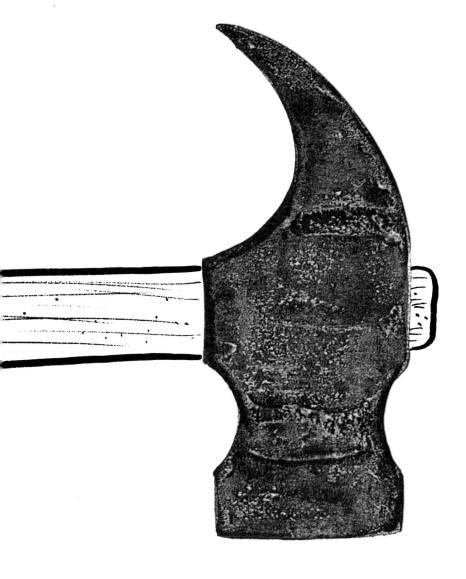

a Hammer
over a Hat

look out, fly!

# I

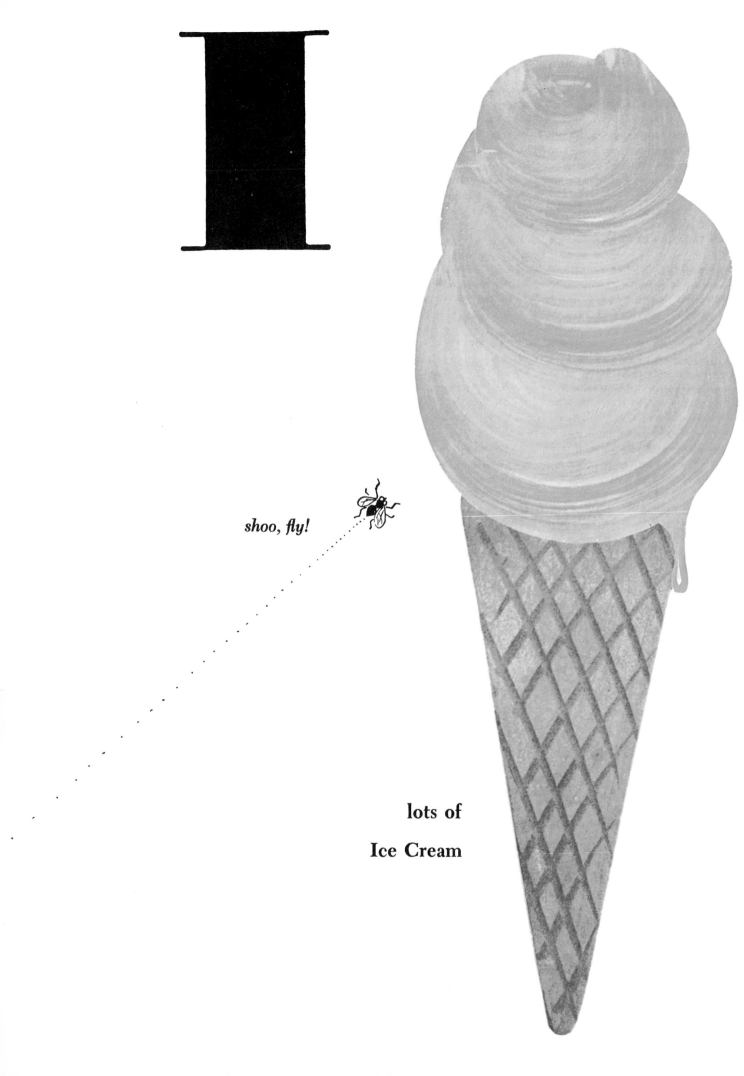

*shoo, fly!*

lots of
**Ice Cream**

a Juggler

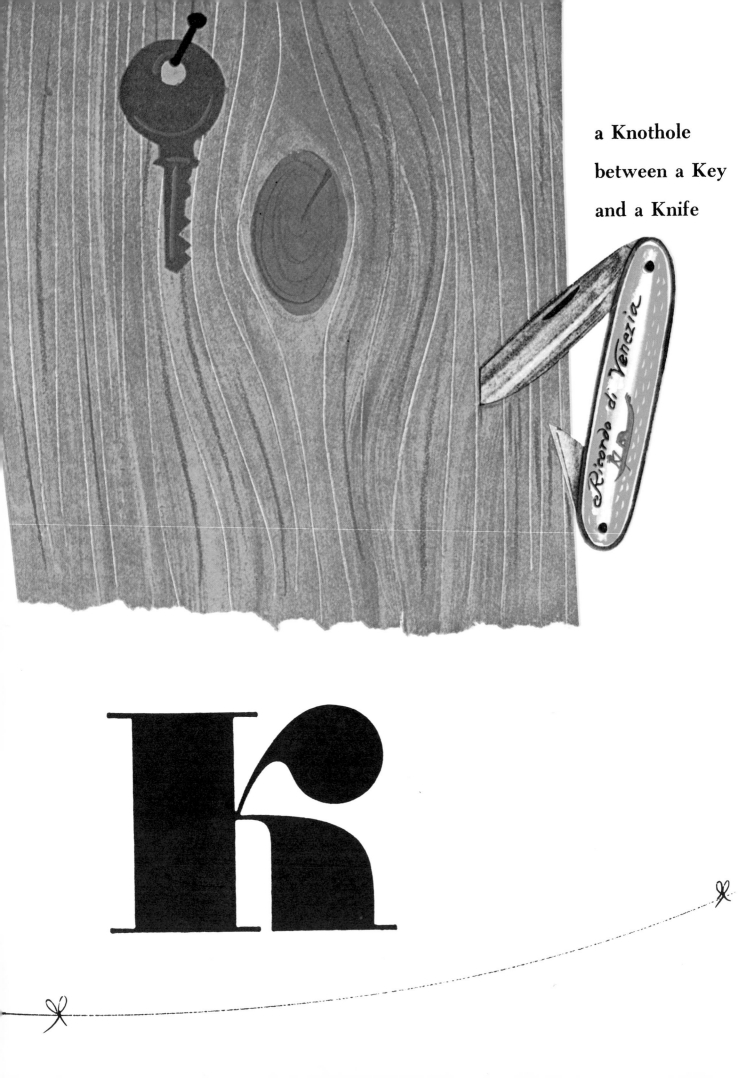

a Knothole
between a Key
and a Knife

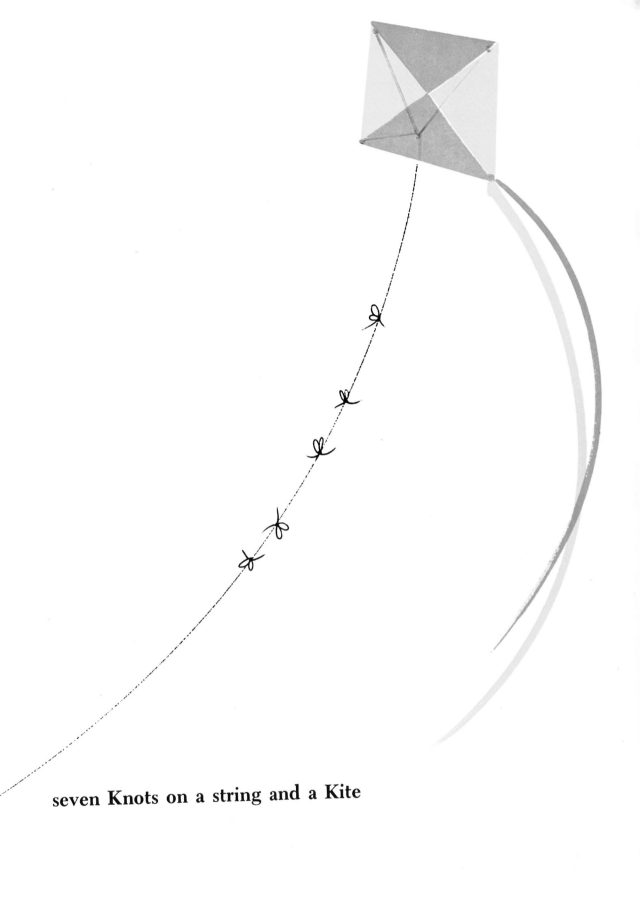

**seven Knots on a string and a Kite**

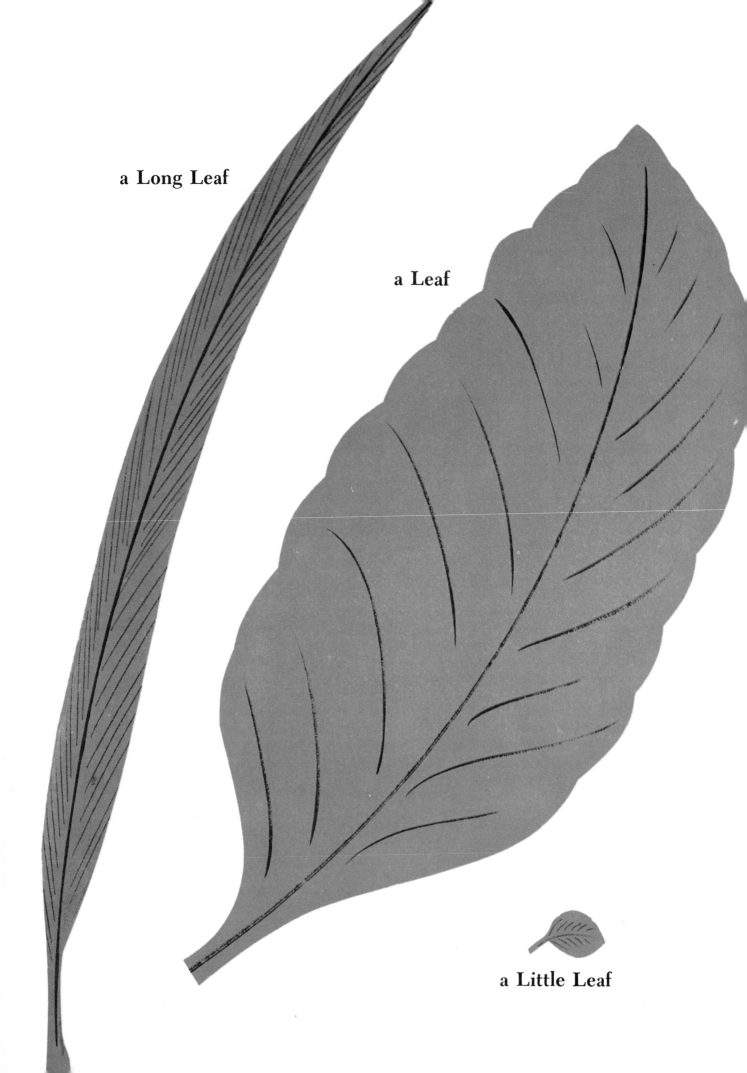

a Long Leaf

a Leaf

a Little Leaf

L

and a Lemon

a Match

M

a Monkey

and a Mouse

No bird in the Nest

N

Nuts on a Nail

an Owl

and an Orange

and an Onion

a Piano

a Package

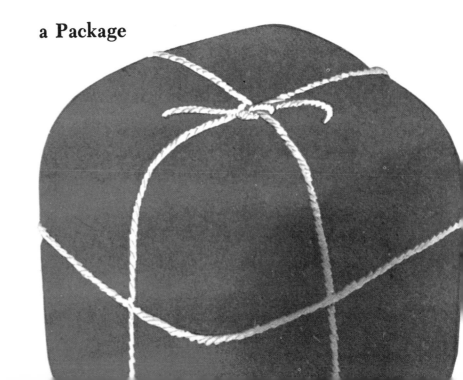

# P

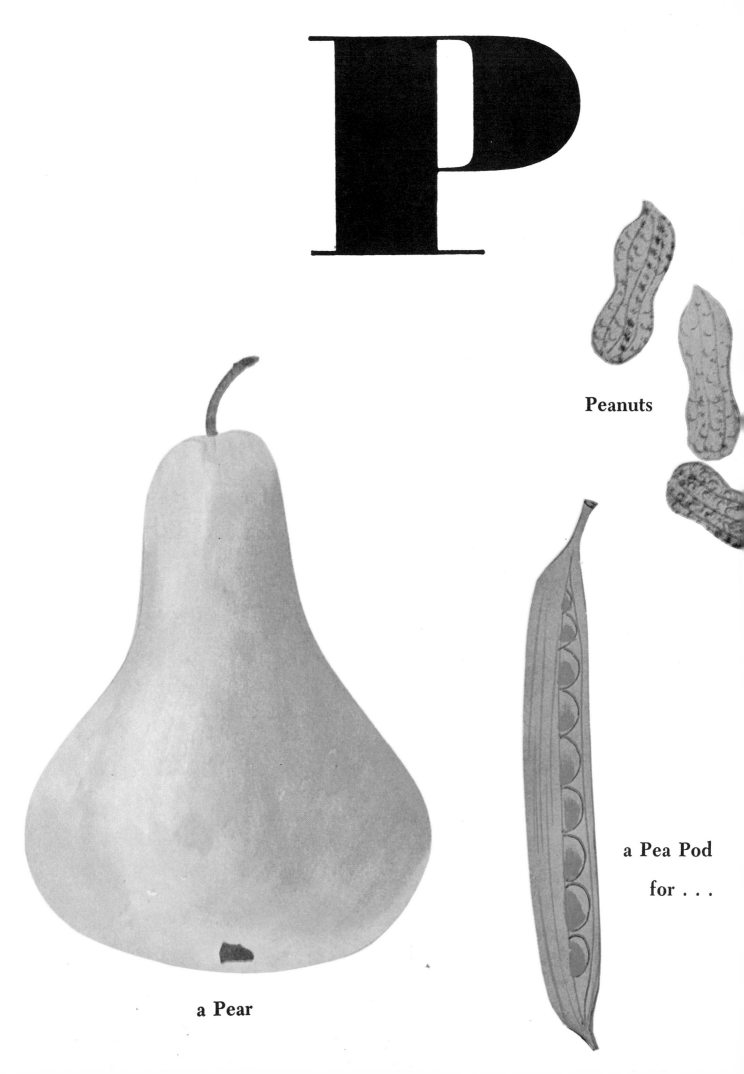

Peanuts

a Pea Pod

for . . .

a Pear

a Quail

R

a Rose

and a Red Ribbon

a Sack
of Stars
and Snow
for
Santa Claus

STOP

and a Sign

all kinds of Shells

even a Ship

and a Stone

**T**

a Trumpet

a Ticket

a Telephone

an Umbrella Up

and an Umbrella

Under the Umbrella

*a fly on a Voyage*

V

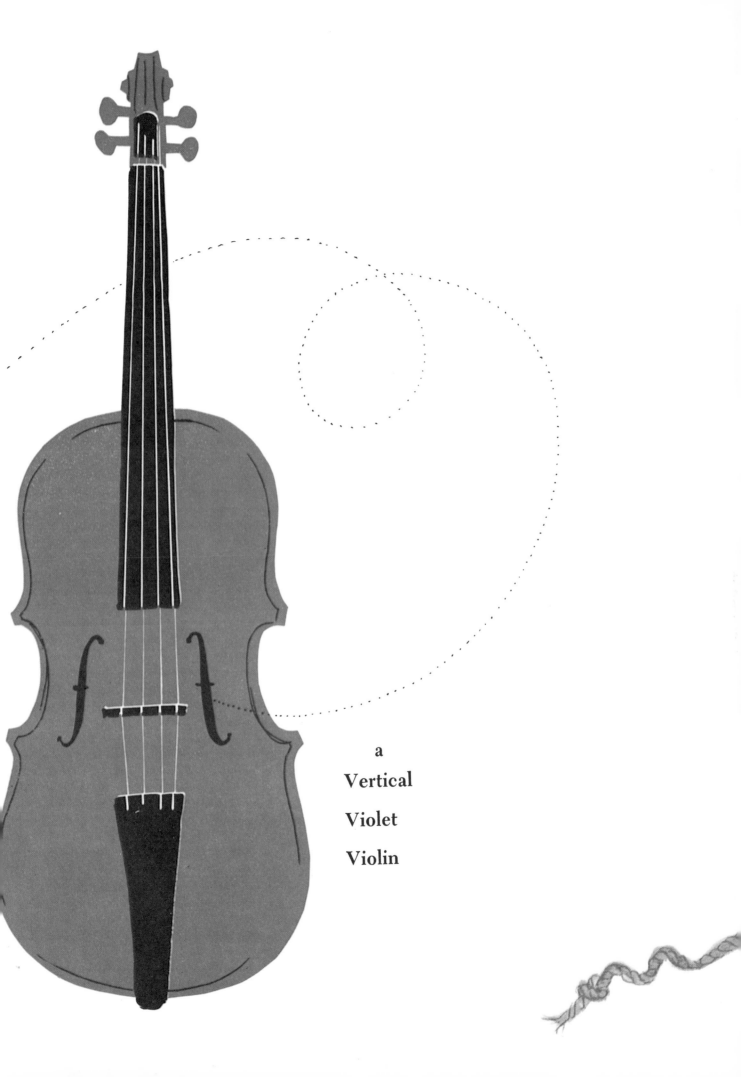

a
Vertical
Violet
Violin

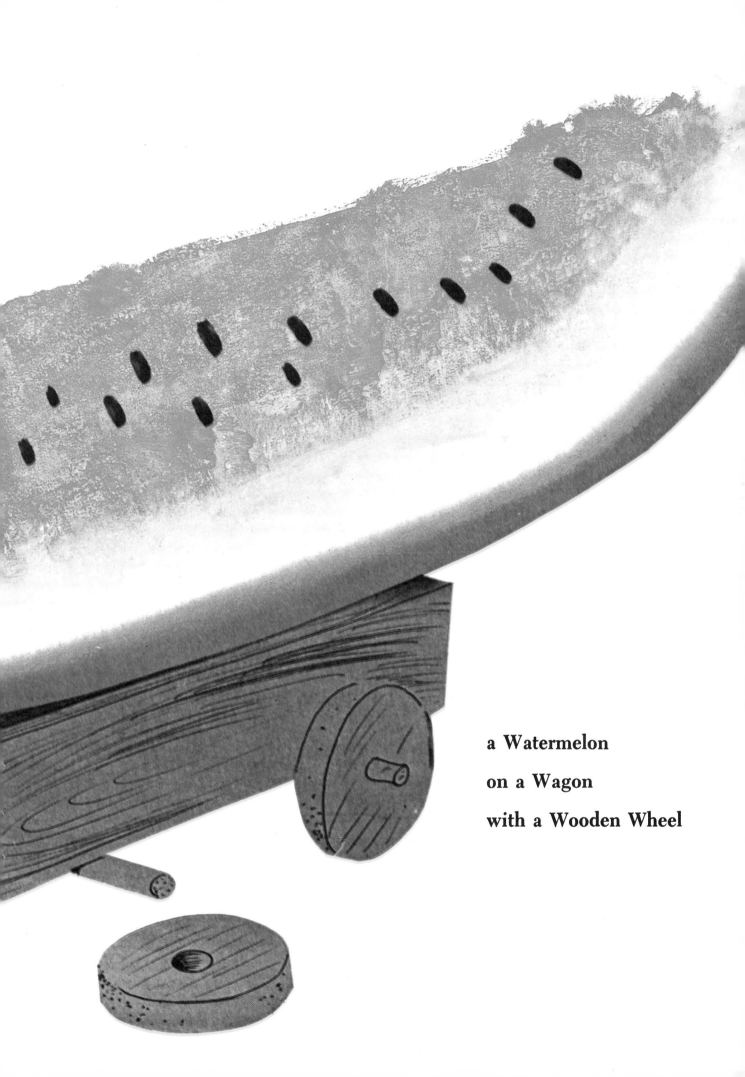

a Watermelon

on a Wagon

with a Wooden Wheel

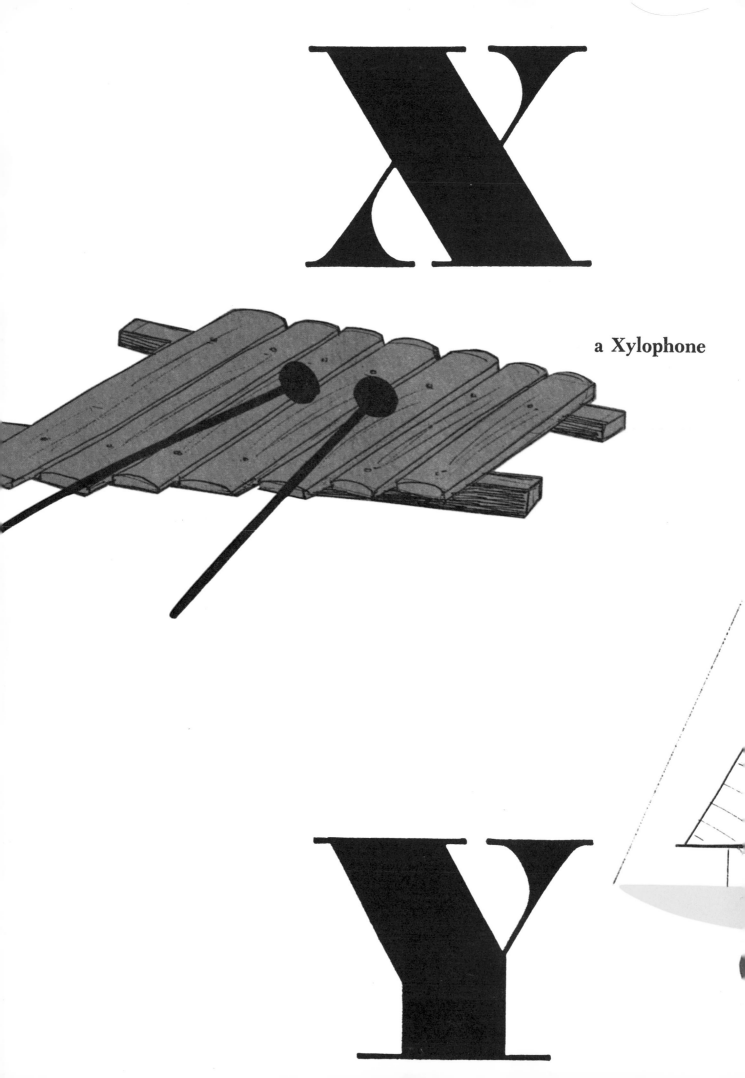

X

a Xylophone

Y

**a Yellow Yacht**

a fly going Zzzz....